D0667171

CANTERLOT HIGH STORIES

CANTERLOT HIGH STORIES

Rainbow Dash
Brings the Blitz

Arden Hayes

LITTLE, BROWN AND COMPANY
New York 𝛺 Boston

This book is a work of fiction. Names, characters, places, and incidents are the product of the author's imagination or are used fictitiously. Any resemblance to actual events, locales, or persons, living or dead, is coincidental.

HASBRO and its logo, MY LITTLE PONY, EQUESTRIA GIRLS and all related characters are trademarks of Hasbro and are used with permission. © 2018 Hasbro. All Rights Reserved.

Cover design by Véronique Lefèvre Sweet.

Hachette Book Group supports the right to free expression and the value of copyright. The purpose of copyright is to encourage writers and artists to produce the creative works that enrich our culture.

The scanning, uploading, and distribution of this book without permission is a theft of the author's intellectual property. If you would like permission to use material from the book (other than for review purposes), please contact permissions@hbgusa.com. Thank you for your support of the author's rights.

Little, Brown and Company
Hachette Book Group
1290 Avenue of the Americas, New York, NY 10104
Visit us at LBYR.com
MLPEG.com

First Edition: April 2018

Little, Brown and Company is a division of Hachette Book Group, Inc.
The Little, Brown name and logo are trademarks of Hachette Book Group, Inc.

The publisher is not responsible for websites (or their content) that are not owned by the publisher.

Library of Congress Control Number 2017956685

ISBNs: 978-0-316-47563-1 (paper-over-board); 978-0-316-47557-0 (e-book)

Printed in the United States of America

LSC-C

10 9 8 7 6 5 4 3 2 1

For Dani

CONTENTS

GIRLS RULE

CHAPTER 1

Beehive Blitzers

"Run, faster, yes, *gooooo*!" Rainbow Dash cried. She stood up, her hands clutched in front of her as she watched the television screen. The Beehive Blitzers, her favorite Blitzball team, were playing in the world championship against BlitzBoom. There were only thirty seconds left in the game.

Lightning Swift, one of the Beehive's fastest players, was dribbling toward the goal.

Applejack peeked out through her fingers. "I don't think I can watch...."

The score was tied, eighteen to eighteen. This one goal would mean winning or going into overtime. Rainbow Dash couldn't bear the thought of a shoot-out. It felt like such a random way to end the season. All that work, for what?

"Yes, you're so close," Rainbow Dash said as Lightning raised his hand, about to shoot the ball into the net. She reached into her pocket and felt for her lucky Beehive key chain. As soon as she'd bought it, the Beehive Blitzers had started winning, and their winning streak hadn't ended since. Just holding it made her feel better.

Everyone in Rainbow Dash's living room held her breath. Lightning took the shot, and one of the BlitzBoomers dove toward it. He reached out his hand, but the ball slipped past his fingers. Everyone cheered as it hit the back of the net.

"Twenty to eighteen!" Applejack threw her arms around Rainbow Dash. "We won!"

Comet Chaser, the Beehive's coach, ran onto the field, and his team enveloped him in a hug. Rainbow Dash and Applejack bounced up and down on their heels. Even Twilight Sparkle did a little dance, excited about the win. Rainbow Dash had known the key chain was a good-luck charm— she'd keep it in a safe place until the following season, when she'd make sure the Beehive Blitzers won again.

Rarity was smiling, but she didn't seem as impressed. She'd spent half the game talking to Fluttershy and Sunset Shimmer about a new dress she was sewing. She was having trouble figuring out what kind of pleats to use on the skirt. Rainbow Dash knew that not all her friends loved Blitzball, and none of them could love it as much as she did, but she'd planned a party for the championship game anyway. She'd served cupcakes with black and gold frosting (the Beehive's colors) and hung a banner over the television. She'd worn her Beehive jersey, the one with Lightning's name and number, and she'd had everyone else wear the team's colors. Rarity would get into the Beehive Blitzers spirit eventually—Rainbow Dash *just knew* she would. Wasn't her excitement contagious?

"The only sad thing is I have to wait a whole eight months before the season starts again," Rainbow Dash said. "What am I going to do with my weekends until then?"

"You can hang out with us," Twilight Sparkle said. "We'll be happy to have you back."

"Was it really that bad?" Rainbow Dash asked.

Fluttershy nodded. "We've barely seen you in the last two months!"

Rainbow Dash blushed. It was true, she had gotten a little obsessed with Blitzball this season. She loved how fast the game moved. The ball was dribbled and passed up the field and shot in the net, then it flew back to the other side of the field. Players stole the ball in really inventive, graceful ways. And the game was totally unpredictable.

Everything could change in an instant, which was so fun to watch.

Lately most of her weekends had been dedicated to watching the league games. Sure, the Beehive Blitzers were her favorite team, but she also loved watching the Larkspurs, the Tiny Titans, and the BlitzBolts. Well, if she were really being honest, she liked watching any team except the Rain Kings. They were the Beehive's biggest rival.

"Great game," Applejack said, grabbing her jean jacket. "Are you wearin' your jersey to school on Monday?"

"You bet," Rainbow Dash said.

"I should get a jersey, too," Sunset Shimmer chimed in. "After that game, I'm officially a Beehive fan. Lightning was all—" She took a few quick steps to the right, then pretended to spike the ball into the net. "It was incredible!"

"A snack for the road..." Pinkie Pie said, taking a cupcake on her way out. "We'll see you Monday, Rainbow Dash!"

When all her friends were gone, Rainbow Dash climbed the stairs to her bedroom. She looked at the three posters on her wall. One was of Lightning Swift, the best player on the Beehive Blitzers. One was of the whole team, and the third was of Oak Arrow, one of her other favorite players.

"Awesome work, guys," she said to them, smiling up at the posters. Then she grabbed the round purple pillow from off her bed. She darted around her room, pretending she was Lightning. She couldn't help wondering what it would be like to be that good

at Blitzball. To weave in and out of the other players, dribbling and ducking, passing and shooting. She ran toward her desk, pretending it was the goal.

"She shoots, she scores!" she yelled, tossing the pillow under the desk. She did a small victory lap with her hands raised high in the air. Then she picked up the pillow, ready to do it all over again.

CHAPTER 2

Go Time

Monday came, and it felt as if Rainbow Dash talked to everyone about the championship game. A boy who sat next to her in chemistry, Forest Thunder, was also a Beehive Blitzer fan. They spent the whole class passing notes back and forth about Lightning, debating over which plays were his best.

Now she was in her last class, the minutes ticking by until the end of the day. Principal Celestia came on the loudspeaker to do the afternoon announcements.

"Congratulations to the girls' track team on their win against Crystal Prep Academy on Friday. Cloudy won the six-hundred-meter dash and..."

Rainbow Dash put her chin in her hands and stared out the window. She could barely pay attention to anything all day. Yesterday she'd started a Beehive Blitzers scrapbook, in which she'd placed news articles and pictures from the whole season. It had taken her forever just to do a few pages, but she couldn't wait to get back to work this afternoon. She'd found this really cool gold foil at the craft store to use behind the photos.

"Rainbow Dash!" Twilight Sparkle said,

nudging Rainbow Dash in the side. "Did you hear that?"

She pointed to the loudspeaker at the front of the room. Principal Celestia went on. "We're obviously thrilled to be part of this amazing opportunity. Now that their season is over, Comet Chaser is bringing Blitzball to students throughout Equestria. Tryouts for his team will be this Friday after school. I hope you're as excited about a Canterlot High Blitzball team as I am."

Rainbow Dash stood up. "Wait…am I dreaming? Did she just say what I think she said?"

"Comet Chaser is coming to our school!" Twilight repeated. "He's starting a program to create a Blitzball high school league!"

"Comet, *the head coach of the Beehive Blitzers*? The first Blitzball player to win MVP in the league?" Rainbow Dash said. "The reason the Blitzers won this season? *One of the toughest players the sport has ever known?*"

"That's him...." Twilight Sparkle smiled.

"You have to try out!" Sunset Shimmer added.

Rainbow Dash couldn't believe it. Comet was a Blitzball legend. Sure, he hadn't played the game in more than a decade, but everyone who knew Blitzball knew his name.

Rainbow Dash grabbed Twilight's hands. She thought she might scream. The only thing better than watching Blitzball would be playing it. For once, she'd have a chance to be part of the action, zipping down the field with the ball, dodging other players as they tried to snatch it from her. She'd have a uniform with her name on the back, with her very own number. Crowds would be cheering, *"Dash! Dash! Rainbow Dash!"*

She straightened up, suddenly serious.

"What's wrong?" Sunset Shimmer asked.

"Friday is only four days away," Rainbow Dash said. "Let's go—I need to practice!"

She grabbed Twilight's and Sunset's hands and they sprinted out of class just as the bell rang. They ran down the hall, heading toward the field.

CHAPTER 3

Mistaken Identity

"One more time!" Applejack called. She held a stopwatch in her hand, with a whistle perched in the side of her mouth. "Ready?"

Rainbow Dash took her place on the far end of the football field. It was a little longer than a Blitzball field was supposed to be, but they'd been using it to practice anyway. The sky was dark. The sun had gone down hours ago, but Applejack and Rainbow Dash were still out on the grass, running drills. Rainbow Dash had been practicing all week. Tryouts were tomorrow and she still didn't feel ready.

"Okay, on the whistle," Rainbow Dash said, clutching the Blitzball in her hand. It was neon blue and just a little smaller than a soccer ball. She stared out at the maze of orange cones in front of her as the shrill sound split the air.

She sprinted as fast as she could, weaving in and out of the cones as if they were players. Applejack had set up a particularly difficult maze at the end of the field and Rainbow Dash ran through it, making sure her footing was light. The first dozen times she'd done it, she'd tripped, but now she moved faster than ever. By the time she got to the end of the field, she was panting.

"Amazin'!" Applejack yelled. She held up the stopwatch. "Twenty-eight seconds! You broke your record!"

Rainbow Dash wanted to cheer or shout, but she was still trying to catch her breath. Applejack handed her water and a towel. After a few minutes, Rainbow Dash smiled.

"Think I'm ready?" she asked, looking at her unofficial coach.

"*Think?*" Applejack said. "I don't *think* you're ready; I *know* you are. You're goin' to wow everyone tomorrow at tryouts."

"Even Comet?"

"Especially Comet."

Rainbow Dash pressed the towel against her forehead. "I wonder who else is going to be there...."

"There was a rumor that Forest Thunder is tryin' out, too," Applejack said. "But other than that, I don't know."

"He's really nice," Rainbow Dash said. Then she noticed Applejack staring at her, her green eyes narrowed. She might as well have said it: *He's your competition!*

Rainbow Dash straightened up, remembering what she was supposed to do.

"He's nice," she repeated, "which is why it'll be sad when I trounce him tomorrow."

"That's the spirit." Applejack smiled. "I cain't wait to watch."

Then she waved Rainbow Dash back onto the field, urging her to do another sprint.

CHAPTER
4

Tricky Tryouts

Rainbow Dash walked over to the bleachers and did a quick spin, showing off the Blitz-ball outfit Rarity had made for her. It was black and gold, the same colors the Beehive Blitzers wore. Rarity had put gold stripes along the shoulders and the sides of the pant legs. The helmet was covered in gold glitter.

"What do you think?" Rainbow Dash asked her friends.

"It's perfect," Applejack said.

"Well, not completely perfect, darling," Rarity admitted. She hopped out of her seat and ran to Rainbow Dash, fixing the stripe on the top of her jersey. The gold ribbon was coming up on one side. Rarity pulled a needle and some thread from her pocket and sewed the ribbon back in place.

Twilight Sparkle, Applejack, Pinkie Pie, Rarity, Sunset Shimmer, and Fluttershy had all come to watch the tryouts. Fluttershy had made little gold-and-black pom-poms that the girls could wave to support Rainbow Dash, while Applejack had brought along a special sports drink and towel that

Rainbow Dash could use whenever she was taking a break. Sunset Shimmer had given her about a dozen pep talks over the last few days, helping her mentally prepare. With friends like these, Rainbow Dash couldn't have been readier.

Rainbow Dash adjusted her helmet, tucking her ponytail underneath it.

"What about now?" She did another spin, holding her arms up in the air.

"You look so tough!" Pinkie Pie squealed.

"I don't even recognize you!" Fluttershy added. She leaned down, peering up under Rainbow Dash's helmet.

The sound of a whistle split the air. Rainbow Dash turned and looked out over the field. A bunch of players were already huddled together in the center. Cones were lined up by the goalposts, and there were about a dozen blue Blitzballs in a pile on the sidelines. Comet strode out onto the field, a whistle in his hand.

"Wish me luck," Rainbow Dash said.

"You've got something better than luck," Sunset Shimmer said. "Talent! You're going to be great."

Rainbow Dash ran out onto the field and got in the huddle just as Comet approached. She thought she recognized Forest Thunder in the back of the group, but it was hard to tell when they were all wearing helmets. Most of the players had borrowed football helmets from the Canterlot High team, but a few had on their own helmets, like Rainbow Dash. They were all wearing numbers on their shirts. Rarity had sewn a giant 22 on Rainbow Dash's jersey, because it had always been her favorite number.

"Blitzball is a game of passion," Comet said, pacing in front of them. "You have to be quick, you have to be slick, but above all you have to have heart. No one can win this game without fierce determination. That's what I'm looking for here today."

The whole group was silent. Rainbow Dash glanced at the crowd, counting the helmets. There were at least twenty people trying out, and there were only ten spots (if you counted the three alternate players. A team usually had seven players, with five on the field at a time). More than half of them would be dismissed by the end of the day.

"I wanted to start a high school Blitzball league because I thought there'd be a lot of young talent, hidden talent, in high schools across this city. I hope you all prove me right."

"You bet we will, Comet!" a boy shouted from the back of the crowd.

Comet ran a hand through his long red hair. "Now, you'll all run a total of five drills today. For the first drill, I need three players on this end of the field and another three down by the goalpost. I want to see what your dribbling and passing skills are like."

After explaining the drills, Comet sat down at a table on the sidelines. Rainbow Dash was part of the first group of players. They ran the length of the field in teams of three, passing and dribbling, dribbling and passing. Rainbow Dash never missed a catch. She never dribbled more than the three times allowed in Blitzball, and every time she passed to one of her teammates, they caught it. She even performed a complicated pass she and Applejack had practiced, where she threw the Blitzball under her leg. It worked!

The rest of the tryouts flew by. Whenever Rainbow Dash wasn't running one of the drills, she was watching the other players closely, trying to pick up different moves from them. She was definitely one of the stronger players, but it was hard to know if Comet had noticed that. Did he see how fast she could sprint? How quick she was with her passes? How she dribbled close to her body so it was harder to steal the ball from her?

When the last drill came, Comet had each of the players run down the length of the field. Other players were stationed at different points to try to steal the ball away from them. All the players lined up by the goalpost, and Rainbow Dash ended up in back.

"This is the hardest drill yet," a boy in front of her said. They watched as a player had his Blitzball knocked right out of his hand. He ended up tripping over one of the cones and wiping out on the grass.

The whistle sounded again, and the boy in front of her darted onto the field. He dodged the first three players who came after him, but then he panicked. He took a hard right to try to get away from the fourth player and ended up smashing into the fifth. They tumbled onto the grass. After a few seconds, they stood up and brushed the dirt off their pants, looking a little dazed.

It was finally Rainbow Dash's turn. Her stomach did somersaults as she waited, listening for the whistle. She stared out at the field, where six different players were stationed, waiting to take the Blitzball from her. She held it tightly in her right hand, her fingers gripping into it. The whistle blared and, without thinking, she sprinted for the other end of the field.

Her greatest strength was her speed. She dribbled past the first two players without any trouble. The third and fourth both got within inches of the Blitzball, but she spun around and did the footwork she and Applejack had practiced, dribbling away. By the time she got to the last two players, she was sure she had it. She faked out the fifth and darted the other way. The last player dove at her, trying to grab the Blitzball, but she sprinted past him and across the other goalpost.

The bleachers erupted in cheers. Rainbow Dash looked up to see her friends standing on the bench, waving their black-and-gold pom-poms. Applejack gave her the thumbs-up.

There was hardly any time to enjoy it, though. Comet was already walking toward them with his clipboard in his hand. He'd been scribbling down notes the whole tryout, rating the players. "Thanks to everyone for coming out today and for giving it your all," he said. "I was impressed by what I saw, and I've decided on the final team."

It was so quiet that Rainbow Dash could hear each of her breaths. The rest of the players were standing perfectly still. The boy beside her was frozen in place, his eyes wide as he waited for Comet to announce his fate.

Comet let out a long sigh, as if he were enjoying making them wait. After another few seconds, he announced it. "Players 54, 33, 96, 101, and 86, you've all made the team."

A few players took off their helmets, shaking out their sweaty hair. Rainbow Dash noticed Forest Thunder was one of the boys who were called. His number was 86.

"Players 43, 52, 97, and 122—you've also made the team."

A few more players pulled off their helmets. They were all boys, too. Rainbow Dash did the math in her head, and her heart raced. There was only one spot left. Why hadn't Comet announced it yet? Was it possible she didn't make it? Hadn't he seen how well she'd played? Why was he making them wait?

"And the last spot goes to player 22.

You showed particular promise on the field. Great sprints, great passes. Consider yourself today's MVP."

Rainbow Dash couldn't help it. She let out a small scream. Then she pulled off her helmet, letting her hair fall down around her shoulders.

She was about to thank him and tell him how much it meant to her to be on this team—*his* team. She wanted him to know she'd been obsessed with Blitzball ever since she found out what Blitzball was. She wanted him to know she'd watched all the clips of him from the Blitzball archives, including the championship game from a decade before, when he'd stolen the ball from Blaze and scored the winning goal. But Comet's eyes were wide. He looked completely in shock.

She glanced around at the rest of the team. They were all boys, and they all looked equally surprised.

"What?" she asked, shrugging. "What's wrong?"

CHAPTER
5

The Big Idea

Comet turned back to the bleachers, where Principal Celestia and Vice Principal Luna were sitting. He narrowed his eyes at them as if they were responsible.

"What?" said Principal Celestia, cooly. "You never said the high school league would be only boys...."

"Well I didn't say that," Comet started, "because I thought it was obvious! Blitzball has always been an all-male sport. In the twenty-year history of the game, there's never been a female player."

"Well, you said it yourself," Vice Principal Luna tried as she followed Principal Celestia out onto the field. "Rainbow Dash was the MVP of tryouts. Don't you think it's time for a change?"

Comet shook his head. "It will throw everything off. One girl...The rest of the players are boys...." He looked at Rainbow Dash again, this time with great disappointment. "No, I'm sorry, you're very good... but no."

Somewhere in the back of the group, a few of the boys who hadn't made the team laughed. Rainbow Dash felt all the blood rush to her face. No one had said she couldn't try out. Sure, maybe the professional Blitzball teams were all men, but she'd just assumed the high school league would be different. Was it silly for her to think that? Was she a fool to dream about playing Blitzball?

"It's not fair, though," a voice said from somewhere behind her.

She turned to see Forest Thunder stepping forward from the group. He held his helmet in his hands. His green eyebrows were pulled together, and he looked upset. "If you never said it was a rule, then she never broke the rule. We'd be lucky to have her on the team, you—"

"Enough," Comet said, holding up his hands. "This is not up for debate. Player 92, congratulations! You'll take 22's place on the team. Player 22, we wish you the best of luck. I'm sure the girls' soccer team would love to have you."

The boys who had been cut were slowly leaving the field. They dropped their stuff in bags and started walking sullenly toward the parking lot. The remaining players scattered into a Blitzball formation. Forest Thunder was the only one who didn't move. He was standing there, waiting for Rainbow Dash to say something.

Whatever embarrassment she felt had already disappeared. Instead she was just angry. For so long she'd dreamed about this moment, about meeting Comet and being on his team. She'd thought he was strong, fierce, and clever. She'd thought he was one of the best Blitzball players in Blitzball history. What she knew now was that he was also kind of a jerk.

"Don't worry about me," she said to Forest Thunder. "I don't want to be on a team that doesn't want me. I'll see you around."

Then she stormed off the field, not even looking at Comet. She didn't stop until she got to the stands, where her friends surrounded her. Pinkie Pie threw her arms around her in a hug.

"This is so unfair," Twilight Sparkle said. "You were the best by far!"

"So rude," Rarity added.

"Comet definitely isn't cool in my book anymore," Sunset Shimmer added. "Not even kind of."

After a moment Principal Celestia and Vice Principal Luna came over to the girls.

Principal Celestia put a hand on Rainbow Dash's shoulder. "I'm sorry, Rainbow Dash," she said. "He never mentioned that only boys could try out for the high school league. I can't control what Comet says or does, but you have every right to petition for a spot."

"Don't be discouraged," Vice Principal Luna said. Then she leaned in and lowered her voice. "I like to think where there's a will, there's a way."

"And if we can help," Principal Celestia said, "you let us know."

Rainbow Dash stared at the boys on the field. They'd already started running their first plays. Comet was ordering them this way and that, yelling for a boy named Ivory to pick up his speed. This was supposed to be *her* big day. That was supposed to be *her* new team.

Twilight Sparkle gave her a hug. "I'm so sorry this is happening," she said.

But Rainbow Dash smiled just a little, watching as the boys darted back and forth.

"Don't be," she said. "I just might have a plan...."

CHAPTER
6

Rules Are Meant to Be Broken

Rainbow Dash strode out onto the field, flanked on either side by her friends. It was the first day of practice for the new Canterlot High Blitzball team, and the boys were already running drills. Rainbow Dash was supposed to be trying out for the girls' soccer team or baking cookies or doing whatever Comet thought she should be doing.

Comet blew the whistle, and all the boys froze in place.

"Speed and agility," he said loudly. "I didn't see either that time. Let's try it again."

"Comet," Rainbow Dash called out to him. "I wanted to talk to you for a second."

Comet spun around. He had a confused look on his face. "What about?"

"You said you couldn't allow a girl in the high school Blitzball league," she said. "But what if your team was stronger with one? Or three? Or coed, with half girls and half boys?"

"Please," Comet said, crossing his arms over his chest. "I don't mean to offend you, but we've already had this discussion.

A coed team just doesn't make sense. The sport has always been all men."

"So you're absolutely certain your team wouldn't be stronger with a few female players?" Twilight Sparkle asked.

Comet tilted his head to the side. He ran his hand through his long red hair. "Yeah, I guess I am."

"Then we challenge you to a game." Rainbow Dash smiled, knowing he'd fallen right into her trap. Now that he'd admitted he didn't think girls were strong Blitzball players, he couldn't say no to playing against them. He wouldn't lose, would he? He seemed to think he couldn't....

"Just a little friendly competition," Rainbow Dash said. "Your team needs to practice for their first game, right?"

"What's the catch?" Comet narrowed his eyes.

"Well, if we win," Rainbow Dash said, "you let me on the team—"

Comet started laughing.

"I'm not finished. You let me on the team *and* you help me create a training program at Canterlot High to recruit girls for Blitzball."

Comet turned back to the boys. They'd all huddled around him, listening to every word Rainbow Dash had said. A boy with striped orange hair shrugged. "Why not?" he asked. "It could be fun to play against a girls' team. It'll keep us on our toes."

Comet shot him a stern look.

"We shouldn't even be having this conversation," an upset Forest Thunder interrupted. He pulled off his helmet and held it in his hands. "She was the MVP of tryouts, remember? She deserves to be on the team."

"But it's an all-boys sport," a freckle-faced kid said.

Comet shook his head, annoyed. Then he turned back to the girls and let out a long sigh. "All right," he said. "Fine. In two weeks, we'll have a scrimmage. Make sure you have seven players ready for a full game. And if you win, you can join the team, but if we win, you have to let us continue the Blitzball season as planned. We can't keep being interrupted with these debates. Rules are rules."

"What's that old saying?" Rainbow Dash asked. She grinned. "Rules are meant to be broken."

Comet didn't seem amused. Instead he turned to the boys, blowing the whistle to get them back into their positions on the field. "Back to work," he yelled. "Let's see those sprints again, this time with more energy and enthusiasm. I need one hundred and ten percent."

As the rest of the boys started the drill, Forest Thunder lingered behind. He gave Rainbow Dash a small smile and wave. It seemed as though he wanted to say something, but then Comet blew the whistle again, and Forest Thunder ran off to join the group.

"I think he likes you...." Sunset Shimmer whispered.

"Who likes who?" Rainbow Dash asked. She turned, wondering if Sunset Shimmer was talking to someone else.

"You, silly," Applejack said, nudging her in the side.

"I think you're imagining it," Rainbow Dash said. Then the boys darted across the field. She glanced over her shoulder one last time to see if Forest Thunder was still watching her, and he was. It was ridiculous, the idea that he liked her, but she did feel better that at least one boy on the team knew they were right. Forest Thunder seemed to think Comet was being as unfair as they thought he was being. Maybe, just maybe, she could count him as a friend.

"Now what do we do?" Pinkie Pie asked. They crossed the parking lot and walked back toward the school.

"Where are you going to find six other players for the girls' team?" Rarity said. She retied the bow on her skirt, making sure it was at the perfect angle.

Rainbow Dash counted her friends one

by one and smiled. "I have my players right here."

Rarity froze in place, as if she weren't quite sure she was hearing correctly. "You're counting me?"

"Yes, I am." Rainbow Dash giggled at Rarity's shocked expression. "We just need to get to work...."

CHAPTER
7

Check Out Receipt

Woodlawn Branch
410-887-1336
www.bcpl.info

Thursday, September 5, 2019 6:26:53 PM
01402

Item: 31183195454860
Title: The narwhal problem
Call no.: First Chapter Book DAD
Due: 09/26/2019

Item: 31183190370772
Title: My little pony : Equestria girls : Canter
lot High stories : Rainbow Dash brings the blitz
Call no.: First Chapter Book MYL
Due: 09/26/2019

Item: 31183191416947
Title: Fairy chase
Call no.: First Chapter Book DAD
Due: 09/26/2019

Total items: 3

You just saved $33.97 by using your
library today.

HOMEWORK HELP

Brainfuse tutoring,
research databases and more
available at bcpl.info

A Secret Mission

"Rarity, you have to run! She's coming for you!" Rainbow Dash called out across the field. Rarity was standing on the grass with the Blitzball tucked under her arm. Her other hand was fixing the strap on her new homemade uniform, complete with glitter tutu. She looked up after Rainbow Dash yelled, as if she were just noticing Twilight Sparkle charging toward her. She started dribbling right away, but it was too late.

"Got it!" Twilight Sparkle easily snatched the ball away from her and held it high in the air. She did a quick victory lap.

"Don't worry about your outfit," Rainbow Dash said. "Next time, just keep the ball in your hands no matter what."

Rarity sat down on the bench and Twilight Sparkle stood in her place. Fluttershy was now sprinting up the field toward her for the next drill. She leaned forward, concentrating as hard as she could, ready to steal the ball. Twilight Sparkle kept adjusting her glasses. This was only their third practice, but her glasses slipped down her nose at the worst moments. She was constantly losing them.

"What do you think?" Rainbow Dash asked. She glanced sideways at Vice Principal Luna as they watched Twilight Sparkle together. Twilight did a quick spin and dribbled away from Fluttershy just as she approached. It wasn't the most incredible Blitzball move Rainbow Dash had ever seen, but they'd only just started.

"They will learn," Luna said. "It's like anything—it just takes time. Not everyone has been practicing Blitzball moves for the past four years."

Vice Principal Luna smiled and gave Rainbow Dash a wink. After Rainbow Dash had challenged Comet to the scrimmage, Vice Principal Luna volunteered to help out as an unofficial coach. She came to every practice after school and stood on the sidelines with the whistle, running drills for

Rainbow Dash. She said nothing made her happier than the thought of Rainbow Dash getting the Blitzball training program she wanted. It would mean dozens of girls learning Blitzball, playing a sport they loved.

"I remember when I helped coach the team for the First Annual Friendship Games," Luna said, watching Pinkie Pie make a few runs. "It's fun seeing how much better everyone gets as the practices go on. The ups and downs of it all…" She stared off and smiled, as if she were remembering something really great.

"Did you win the Games that year?" Rainbow Dash asked.

"We did," Vice Principal Luna said. "It was a little complicated, but we were given the trophy. That Friendship Games was one of the reasons I joined the soccer team my sophomore year. It's when I really fell in love with sports."

"Well, I'm definitely in love with Blitz-ball," Rainbow Dash said.

Vice Principal Luna laughed. "I know you are."

Luna checked her watch, then handed the whistle to Rainbow Dash. "It seems like you have everything under control here, so I'm going to head back to the office. Just a reminder—I'll have to miss the rest of this week's practices because of parent-teacher conferences. I'll see you Monday, though."

Monday...Rainbow Dash thought. *By then the game will be five days away. Will we really be ready? How can I be sure I'm training them right, when I've never officially trained a team?*

"Don't look so worried!" Vice Principal Luna said. "You girls are going to be great."

"I hope you're right," Rainbow Dash said.

"Of course I'm right," Vice Principal Luna called over her shoulder as she walked off. She gave Rainbow Dash a wave.

Rainbow Dash turned and ran onto the field, blowing the whistle a few times. "Okay, team!" she yelled. "One last drill before we wrap up today—three-on-four!"

"We probably shouldn't be on the same team," Sunset Shimmer said, looking at Rainbow Dash. She'd gotten the hang of Blitzball the fastest. After only three practices, she was a total natural.

"Probably not," Rainbow Dash said, knowing that they'd be too strong a team together. "How about you go with Rarity,

Fluttershy, and Twilight Sparkle? Pinkie Pie and Applejack—you'll be on my team."

The girls lined up on either side of the white chalk line. Because the boys were practicing on the football field, they had to use the soccer field in the back of the school. It was a little smaller than a Blitzball field, and the lines weren't right, but it did the trick. They'd heard a rumor they were going to make a Blitzball field by the forest behind the school. Rainbow Dash had kept looking for signs they'd started. . . .

"Let's pretend we're in possession of the Blitzball," Rainbow Dash said, passing it to Applejack. "We'll start on this whistle."

Once you had the Blitzball, all you had to do was run it toward the goal. There were no goalies—just defense. You could dribble only three times before passing, but you could stop and spin around, changing positions to get away from whoever was trying to block you. You needed your teammates, and you needed to learn different strategies for getting away from your opponents. The game was supposed to move ten times faster than they'd been playing it, but Rainbow Dash hoped they'd speed up eventually.

Applejack held the ball in her hands. Rainbow Dash was standing to the right of her, and Pinkie Pie was to Applejack's left. The other team was ready to pounce as soon as the whistle blew. Rainbow Dash knew she'd have to be quick if she was going to get the ball anywhere close to the goal. She blew the whistle and sprinted as fast as she could, holding her hands up for the pass.

Applejack was one of the stronger players, and she was able to dribble three times before Sunset Shimmer was right beside her. Sunset waved her arms around, trying to block the pass, but Applejack threw it low to the ground. Rainbow Dash caught it just before it hit the grass!

She turned to throw to Pinkie Pie, but Pinkie Pie was off goofing around with Twilight. She was doing some kind of fancy footwork, trying to get Twilight to laugh, but then she tripped and they both fell on the ground. Twilight's glasses slipped off again, and she was feeling around for them.

Rarity was slowly jogging toward her, taking long, dainty steps in her cleats. Rainbow Dash decided she'd try to get as close to the goal as possible and then just throw it as far and as fast as she could. She'd seen Oak do this move a hundred times before—it was called "the beesting."

"*Ummm*…you'd better watch out.…" Fluttershy said uncertainly, stepping in front of her. She'd been behind Rainbow Dash, so she hadn't noticed her at first. "This Blitzball is not getting by me today, no way, no how…"

But she said it so softly it wasn't convincing. Fluttershy hated reaching for the ball or trying to steal it away. Rainbow Dash dribbled once, then twice, and Fluttershy seemed confused about what to do. She glanced sideways at Rarity, but Rarity just shrugged.

Rainbow Dash wanted to help them, she did, but they were supposed to be on the opposite team. They were her *opponents*. She dribbled once more and then threw the ball as hard as she could toward the net.

Fluttershy didn't try to intercept it—instead she jumped out of the way. As soon as the other side scored, she seemed relieved it was all over.

"Let's hope practice really does make perfect," Rainbow Dash said.

"Same time and same place tomorrow?" Applejack said, helping up Twilight Sparkle and Pinkie Pie.

"You got it," Rainbow Dash said.

"I just have to find a good cord for my glasses…." Twilight Sparkle said to no one in particular. Then she walked off the field, the others following behind her. Applejack stayed to help Rainbow Dash bring the supplies back to the gym.

"They're still learning," Rainbow Dash said hopefully. "We still have a full week and a half before the scrimmage. We'll be fine."

Applejack waited until the girls were halfway across the parking lot before she said anything. "I wasn't sure if I should tell you this...but there's a rumor goin' 'round that the boys' team is...well, that they're really good."

"Who said that?" Rainbow Dash asked, pulling the bag of Blitzballs along behind her. Applejack picked up a few cones.

"Everyone..." Applejack said. "Apparently people have been watchin' their practices on the football field. They've been doin' two practices every day. One right after school and one at night, under the lights."

"Two practices?!" Rainbow Dash asked. She hadn't even thought of that. They'd been ending every day at six, and even *she* thought that was a lot.

"Yeah…" They walked quietly toward the gym, pulling the supplies behind them.

Rainbow Dash tried to seem as if she didn't care, as if she were just as confident as before. But she was starting to worry. She kept thinking her friends would get better, but what if they didn't? What if Fluttershy was still afraid of the ball next week? And Twilight Sparkle was still nervous about her glasses breaking? And Rarity kept fidgeting with her outfit? And Pinkie Pie kept goofing around during plays?

"Why don't we come back tonight?" Rainbow Dash finally said. "If they're really that good, we should see for ourselves."

"I think we should…" Applejack nodded as they loaded the Blitzballs and cones into the gym closet.

CHAPTER 8

Smarter, Faster, Fiercer

"Be careful," Rainbow Dash said, waving for Applejack to follow her. She was hiding behind a tree near the football field. Applejack was one tree behind her. They'd been running from tree to tree, getting closer and closer to the field, but Rainbow Dash was nervous someone would see them.

They'd look like spies, trying to suss out the competition (maybe that *was* what they were doing, but still).

Applejack peered out from behind the tree, then sprinted as fast as she could to Rainbow Dash. They were just a short distance from the bleachers now. If they moved fast while the team was running drills, no one would notice as they went underneath the stands. From there they'd have a good view of the entire field.

Comet's booming voice split the air. "I want everyone to improve their sprints by ten seconds," he said. "That's the goal for next week. And everyone should be able to execute the under/over block perfectly."

"The under/over block? What is that?" Rainbow Dash whispered. She'd never even heard of it.

As soon as Comet blew the whistle for the drill, the girls sprinted toward the bleachers. They crouched down behind one of the lowest benches and peered out below it. From where they were, they had a perfect view of the field. The boys raced across it as Comet timed them.

"They're really fast," Applejack said. "They're twice as fast as Sunset Shimmer, at least."

"And their footwork is pretty good, too," Rainbow Dash said. She'd used the words *pretty good*, but she really meant *incredible*. For the second drill, they sprinted down the field, weaving in and out of cones. They turned around at the midfield point and started running backward, but that didn't slow them down one bit.

And then there was the famous under/over

block. They did it a few drills after, but it was obvious what it was, because it was one of the more impressive moves they had. A player would come dribbling down the field, and the offense would do a series of fake outs. They would throw their hands up, then down, or vice versa. But when the player passed the ball, they were always right there. They always caught it right away. The move made it impossible to know if it was better to pass to the side or over the players' heads. You just couldn't predict what they were going to do.

"Well, call me a moldy apple, because there's no way we're not gettin' squished!" Applejack said, watching as Forest Thunder slammed a Blitzball out of another boy's hands.

Rainbow Dash wanted to tell her she was wrong, that they'd be fine. But she couldn't stop picturing what their practices looked like. How many passes they'd dropped, how slow Rarity was when she moved across the field. It was as if she weren't in the middle of a competitive game.

Then there was Pinkie Pie, with all her jokes and gags. And Fluttershy, who refused to steal the ball away from anyone, because she thought it was kind of mean . . .

"We have to come up with a better strategy," Rainbow Dash said, turning to Applejack. "Too much is at stake. We can't afford to lose."

Applejack was still staring straight ahead. She couldn't stop watching the practice. A boy with striped hair had passed the ball, rolled on the grass, and caught it again. Comet kept blowing the whistle, over and over, and yelling out new drills. It was already nine o'clock, and from the way it looked, they'd be practicing all night.

"We need to be so much faster, smarter, and fiercer..." Applejack said. "But how are we goin' to do that, when the game is only a week and a half away?"

CHAPTER 9

Practice Makes Perfect

Rainbow Dash rubbed her eyes and tried to stifle a yawn. She walked onto the soccer field with Applejack, watching as their team set up the cones for the first drills. Applejack held a rolled-up piece of paper under her arm.

"Hold on, Pinkie. You don't need to do

that," Rainbow Dash said. She pointed to the cones Pinkie Pie was arranging in a line. "We're going to do things a little bit differently today. Team—come in for a huddle!"

All her friends gathered around her. Rarity was wearing a new Blitzball outfit she'd sewn the night before, trying to get it just right. This one had a bright blue tutu and leggings, with glittery gold high-top cleats. Rainbow Dash had to admit—it was the cutest of all the outfits Rarity had come up with, but it didn't look very comfortable. Rainbow Dash's tryout outfit seemed like the only design that was practical enough for the sport.

Applejack knelt and unrolled the piece of paper on the grass. The girls leaned forward, studying all the tiny *X*s and *O*s drawn in different places. There was a list of funny phrases most of them hadn't ever seen before: The "spinning grab," "sticky fingers," and "leaping lizard" were just a few.

"Rainbow Dash and I have some intel," Applejack said.

"Intel?" Pinkie Pie laughed loudly. "Is that some sort of code word?"

"That just means we got some secret information we probably shouldn't have," Applejack said. "We found out the boys' team is...well, they're good. They're really good. And we need to get really good right quick if we're going to have any chance of beatin' them."

"Which is why we came up with these new plays." Rainbow Dash pointed to the paper. "Applejack and I were up late working on these. New plays and new moves to bring our team to the next level."

"We have five different plays that we can use together, as a team," Applejack explained. "And then Rainbow Dash and I came up with new moves that we should all practice until they're perfect. They could give us a real competitive edge."

Her friends crowded together, studying the paper as Applejack explained the first play. It involved two of the teammates flanking the first runner as she took off up the field. There was a fake pass, a decoy runner, and then a second fake pass. Rainbow Dash smiled as Applejack described how the final runner would score the goal.

Coming up with inventive plays was so much fun. It was easy for Rainbow Dash; she just didn't know why she hadn't thought of it sooner. All those afternoons watching

Blitzball had made her an expert on the game. She had practiced so many weird moves and fake outs in her bedroom— now she just had to teach them to her friends. With a little help, they could be just as good as the boys' team; she knew they could.

"What is that one?" Fluttershy asked. She pointed to the biggest play on the paper, a series of *X*s and *O*s and arrows going in different directions.

"That's the 'colossus'," Applejack said. "It's our biggest move. By the end of our practices, we need to have that one down perfectly. Picture this…" She spread her hands apart, as if she were imagining a television screen in front of her. "The score is tied. We're in control of the ball, and we only have one play left, or the game goes into a shoot-out. The tension in the air is so thick you could cut it with a knife. What do we do?"

"We use the 'colossus'!" cheered Pinkie Pie, jumping up and down.

"That's exactly right," Rainbow Dash said. "It's our secret weapon."

"What is a 'leaping lizard'?" asked Sunset Shimmer, reading off the paper.

"Oh, that's one of my favorites...." Rainbow Dash grabbed a Blitzball from the pile and tossed it to Applejack. "I'll show you; I just need someone to block me."

Sunset Shimmer jogged onto the field and faced off against Rainbow Dash, throwing up her arms so Applejack couldn't pass to her. But as soon as Rainbow Dash had the chance, she took three quick steps to the right and leaped dramatically into the air. When she was clear, Applejack threw the ball to her. Rainbow Dash caught it in midair!

"That was awesome!" Pinkie Pie cried.

"Why's it called the 'leaping lizard'? Do you have to stick out your tongue or something?" Twilight Sparkle asked.

"We just wanted to give it a funny name," Applejack said. "But sure, you can stick out your tongue, too."

Twilight Sparkle readjusted her glasses. Then she took a few quick steps to the right and jumped. Rainbow Dash threw her the ball, but she panicked at the last minute and put one hand on her glasses, holding them in place. The Blitzball bounced off her arm and hit the ground.

"That was...sort of it," Applejack tried.

Rainbow Dash looked at Applejack and shrugged. "Let's get to practicing," she said. "We have a lot to learn, and the scrimmage is almost a week away...."

CHAPTER
10

Breaking Points

"No, no, no, no, no," Rainbow Dash said under her breath. She couldn't believe what was happening. Fluttershy was right by the goal, and Sunset Shimmer was standing with the ball, right within reach. The Blitzball couldn't have been more than six inches from her hand, but Fluttershy still didn't reach out and grab it.

Sunset Shimmer sprinted past and threw the Blitzball into the net. Pinkie Pie and Rarity, who were both on her team, raised their arms in the air and cheered.

"Why won't she just steal the ball from her?" Rainbow Dash said out loud. "I don't understand why it's so hard. It was right there."

It was Monday afternoon, and Vice Principal Luna was back at practice. She stood next to Rainbow Dash on the edge of the field as the two teams faced off against each other. They watched as Fluttershy apologized to her teammates, Applejack and Twilight Sparkle.

"Just show her again," Vice Principal Luna said. "See if you can get her to take it

from you. There's nothing to be scared of—
it's part of the game."

Rainbow Dash trotted out onto the field.
She tried to seem as if she weren't annoyed,
but three whole practices had passed since
she showed her team the new plays and they
hadn't mastered them the way she'd wanted
them to. On Monday they'd go up against the
boys' team, and they still weren't ready. They
barely had any time left to practice.

Fluttershy held up her hands as soon as
she saw Rainbow Dash. She looked as if she
might cry. "I'm sorry. I was going to grab it,
I was, but then she got away from me...."

"You don't have to say sorry," Rainbow
Dash said. "Let's just try it again. There's
not even a second to hesitate in Blitzball.
You just have to go for it."

Rainbow Dash grabbed a ball off the

ground and dribbled it past Fluttershy. "See, I'm right within reach. Just swipe it. How about the 'crab claw' move we showed you?"

Fluttershy looked nervous. She ducked down, then grabbed the ball with one hand and locked her other arm around it. But when it was time for her to yank it away from Rainbow Dash, she couldn't do it.

"What's wrong?" Rainbow Dash asked. "Just pull it away."

"I don't know...." Fluttershy let go of the ball. "It just seems kind of...mean."

"It's the game!" Applejack called from across the field. "It's what we have to do to *win*!"

It was obvious Fluttershy couldn't do it, though. Instead of wasting time, Rainbow Dash moved to the next play they'd been practicing over and over again.

"How about the 'colossus'?" she said. "Let's run it a few times."

They'd run it a dozen times, but they still hadn't gotten it to work. Rainbow Dash was trying to stay positive, but it seemed as if something always went wrong. Twilight Sparkle's glasses slipped off and fell, or Pinkie Pie was goofing around and missed her cue. Rainbow Dash was hoping this time would be different. It *really* needed to be different....

"Rarity, Sunset Shimmer, Pinkie Pie, and Applejack," she said. "You'll run it together. Sunset, you'll have the ball. Rarity, you'll be in position for the scoring goal. Pinkie Pie and Applejack, you'll flank Sunset on either side. Everyone else, let's pretend we're on Comet's team!"

Rainbow Dash joined all her friends on

the other side of the field, ready to stop the "colossus" any way they could. Even when you knew the play was coming, it was hard to figure out how to counter it. When they played the boys, they'd have the element of surprise.

Rainbow Dash blew the whistle and Sunset Shimmer ran up the center, flanked by Pinkie Pie and Applejack. Pinkie Pie and Applejack darted to opposite sides of the field and Sunset Shimmer passed to Applejack, who tossed to Rarity so she could score. Only Rarity wasn't looking. Her tutu had come undone, and she was struggling to tie the bow again. The Blitzball whizzed past her and went out of bounds.

The worst part was, Rarity didn't even notice what had happened. When she finally looked up, Applejack had to explain that she'd missed the ball.

Rarity shrugged. "I'm sorry, darling. I just didn't realize we were—"

"The game is coming up in no time!" Rainbow Dash interrupted. As soon as she spoke the words, she couldn't stop herself. All her frustration from the past week came spilling out. "We're nowhere close to ready. Forget a training program—we're going to make complete fools of ourselves. Why can't you take this seriously?!"

She looked at her friends. They were all frozen, watching her, completely stunned. She knew she was mad, and maybe it had come out a little harsh, but she didn't care. How could she when so much was at stake? When the whole school had been talking about the

game against the boys and how she'd challenged Comet to the scrimmage? Why didn't
anyone else care as much as she did?

Before her friends could say anything,
she stormed off the field, not bothering to
look back.

CHAPTER 11

New Attitudes

Rainbow Dash didn't stop walking until she got to the Wondercolt statue in front of the school. She sat down and leaned against it. Why didn't her friends understand how important this game was to her and all the girls? Did they really want everyone to see them get beaten by a bunch of boys? Didn't they know how much was at stake? She'd challenged Comet, one of the most famous coaches in Blitzball history, to a scrimmage against *his* team. And for what? To lose in front of the entire school?

"I can't believe this," she said to herself, putting her face in her hands. "What did I do?"

"Mind if I sit down?" asked a familiar voice.

Rainbow Dash looked up and saw Vice Principal Luna standing beside the statue. She pointed to the patch of grass next to Rainbow Dash, then sat down beside her and crossed her legs.

"You seemed pretty upset back there," Vice Principal Luna said gently. "Want to talk about it?"

Rainbow Dash felt the blood rush to her cheeks. Maybe she shouldn't have yelled at her friends, but she couldn't help it. They'd been practicing for a week and a half and they'd made zero progress. They were still making all the same silly mistakes they'd made on the very first day!

"I think I was too optimistic," Rainbow Dash said. "I just assumed we'd be able to pull it together for game day, but what if we can't? I feel like the whole school is going to see it as a reason to never let girls on the Blitzball team. Ever. That would be terrible...."

Vice Principal Luna let out a deep, slow breath. "That *would* be terrible," she repeated. Rainbow Dash had always thought Luna had one of the kindest faces. She had big green eyes and long purple hair that fell past her shoulders. She was one of those people who always seemed to be smiling, even when she wasn't.

"And it would be all my fault...." Rainbow Dash added.

"No, not at all. It's wrong that you weren't allowed on the Blitzball team," said Vice Principal Luna. "I went to the tryouts and I saw how well you played, and Comet hadn't made any official rules about not letting girls on the team. It was just wrong. You never should have been in this position to begin with."

"But what does that matter?" Rainbow Dash asked.

"I'm proud of you, that's all," Vice Principal Luna said. "You stood up for yourself.

And you stood up to someone who was treating you unfairly. That's really something."

"Thanks," Rainbow Dash said. "It still doesn't change the fact that we're not even close to ready for Friday...."

"The team will figure it out," Vice Principal Luna said. "But for now, you owe your friends an apology. They're all doing the best they can, and being a good coach means recognizing that, no matter what."

Rainbow Dash nodded, knowing Vice Principal Luna was right. Two weeks ago, none of her friends had even played Blitzball, and now she was teaching them complicated moves and expecting them to do them perfectly.

"I guess I have been pretty hard on them...." Rainbow Dash admitted. "I'll be sure to tell them how much I appreciate them."

"And remember—this is supposed to be fun," Vice Principal Luna said with a wink. "What's the point of playing if you're not enjoying yourself?"

Vice Principal Luna stood and offered Rainbow Dash her hand. As they walked back toward the field, Rainbow Dash couldn't stop thinking of how she'd yelled at her friends. Of course Twilight Sparkle worried about her glasses—she'd broken them in gym last year playing volleyball, and she'd had to manage without them for a whole week while they were getting fixed. And maybe Fluttershy was a bit timid on the field, but wasn't her kindness what made her such a good friend? Hadn't that been the thing Rainbow Dash loved most about her?

Then there was Rarity. She'd spent two whole nights working on Rainbow Dash's outfit for her tryouts. She'd made sure it was sleek and stylish and perfect for playing Blitzball. Was it so wrong that she'd been trying out different styles on the field?

The more Rainbow Dash thought about it, the worse she felt. Her stomach twisted in knots as they turned the corner to the field. She'd tell them she was sorry.

But when they got to the field, it was empty except for the Blitzball equipment. All her friends were gone. Even Applejack had left, not bothering to help her clean up.

"They must have gone home already," Vice Principal Luna said delicately, seeing

Rainbow Dash's expression. "They'll be back tomorrow...."

Rainbow Dash tried to smile, but she wasn't so sure. Why would her friends come back when she'd been so hard on them? Or had today been the last time her team played together?

CHAPTER
12

Friends and Teammates

The next day, Rainbow Dash was in history class with Applejack and Rarity, but it seemed as if every time she was going to apologize, they got interrupted. First by their teacher Ms. Pansy, then by the bell. She saw Twilight Sparkle in between classes, but it was only for a minute, and Twilight Sparkle didn't even mention Blitzball. As the day was coming to an end, she kept wondering if she'd be the only one at practice.

To make everything worse, about a dozen people came up to her to tell her they were coming to the game. A freshman girl said she was so excited that she was making posters, and another group of girls peppered her with a million questions. Did they know when the training program would start? How many girls would they let in it? Had they come up with a name for their team yet?

By the time the last bell rang, she felt sick. She went to the gym closet after school and grabbed the Blitzballs. Applejack didn't come meet her. She saw Rarity across the parking lot with her backpack on and a huge box in her arms, as if she were going somewhere else. As Rainbow Dash brought the supplies out to the field, she kept running what had happened through her head. Had she gone too far yesterday? Was everyone mad and just not telling her?

As she turned the corner toward the field, her heart leaped. All her friends were there. They were all in matching outfits— the same one Rarity had made for her tryouts. And they were running the "colossus." Applejack and Vice Principal Luna were coaching them.

Rainbow Dash watched as Twilight Sparkle raced up the field with the ball in her hand. She spun around, passing to Sunset Shimmer, who passed to Rarity. Rarity wasn't even paying attention to her new outfit. She was too busy dribbling and scoring. Rainbow Dash raised her arms and cheered as the ball hit the back of the net.

When she got to her friends, they surrounded her. They were smiling and warm, and her stomach sank thinking about what she had done. "I'm so sorry about what I said yesterday, I—"

"You were right, though. We weren't taking it seriously enough," Twilight Sparkle said. She pointed to her glasses, which were now covered with thick plastic goggles. There didn't seem to be a chance they'd break. "I borrowed these goggles from the bio department. Now I don't have to worry about my glasses falling off or snapping."

"And you were right, darling," Rarity said. "Maybe tutus aren't the *best* idea for a Blitzball outfit. What do you think of our new uniforms?"

"I love them," Rainbow Dash said warmly.

"I thought they were so comfortable, too. That outfit really helped me play my best."

"And watch!" Fluttershy said, stealing a Blitzball from underneath Sunset Shimmer's arm. "I practiced all night."

Rainbow Dash laughed. "You're getting really good at that!" She looked around at her team, so thankful they were still here for her. "I want you to know, no matter what happens on Friday, I'm really lucky to have you all as friends. Some of you hadn't even touched a Blitzball before last week. As long as we give it our all and try our best, I'll be happy with however it turns out."

"We're not going to just try our best," Pinkie Pie said. "We're going to win!"

She weaved in and out of cones on the field, sprinting faster than Rainbow Dash had ever seen her run. Applejack leaned over and smiled. "I ran my own late practice last night to try to get them into shape for you."

"It worked," Rainbow Dash said. "How about we try the 'three S's'? Pinkie Pie, Sunset Shimmer, and Fluttershy, you're up!"

The girls ran into formation and started weaving up the field, making three giant S shapes. Applejack was right. They looked faster and stronger than they'd ever been. And more than anything, they looked as if they were playing with their whole hearts. Fluttershy whizzed past, barely noticing that the others were watching her.

If we give it our all, Rainbow Dash thought, *we might actually win. . . .*

CHAPTER 13

The GlitzyBlitzers

Rainbow Dash walked out onto the field to applause. A few dozen Canterlot High kids had come out for the game against the boys' team. It was mainly groups of freshman and sophomore girls, some waving signs and others shaking blue-and-gold pom-poms. Word had spread that Rainbow Dash had stood up to Comet, and she'd become a legend of sorts. Girls would whisper as she passed in the halls, and others had started watching Blitzball, arguing about who would win next season. As she looked up into the stands at all their smiling faces, Rainbow Dash tried not to worry. What if she let them down?

"You girls are going to do great," Vice Principal Luna said. They huddled around her on the side of the field, glancing over to the boys across the way. Forest Thunder and his team were sitting on the bench, downing the last of their sports drinks.

"We did all we could," Twilight Sparkle said. "We couldn't be more ready."

It was true. They'd done three late-night practices in the days leading up to the game. They'd run every play until they'd had it down perfectly, and Rainbow Dash had even taken the extra time to make sure Fluttershy was comfortable with different kinds of steals, even the trickier ones. In that short time, the girls had all gotten their sprint times down by a few seconds. They were as fast as they were ever going to be.

"I feel good," Applejack said. Then she glanced sideways at Rainbow Dash and smiled.

"You look good, too," Rarity added, "if I do say so myself." She'd spent her lunch period sewing their team name onto the jerseys. They'd decided on the name *the GlitzyBlitzers*, and now it was embroidered on their backs in gold.

Orange Haze, the bio teacher who'd lent Twilight Sparkle her goggles, had volunteered to be the ref. He blew the whistle, calling the teams to the center of the field. Rainbow Dash pointed for everyone except Rarity and Pinkie Pie to follow her. They were so used to practicing against one another, using teams of three and four, she hoped nothing changed when they played against the boys. Now it would be five on five, the teams evenly matched.

Rainbow Dash called her team into a huddle. She cleared her throat, trying to ignore the butterflies swirling around her stomach. "Just remember," she said, "give it your all. Everything you have. We've come such a long way... now let's go a little further. We can do this; I know we can."

"Go, team GlitzyBlitzers!" Sunset Shimmer yelled.

"Go, GlitzyBlitzers!" the other girls repeated.

They jogged to the center of the field

and took their positions across from Forest Thunder and the other boys. Rainbow Dash had won the coin toss back in the gym, so their team had the ball first. She tucked it under her arm and looked up into Forest Thunder's eyes. She was expecting him to glare back at her, ready to win, but instead he looked different... strange.

"Are you okay?" she asked.

He had dark circles underneath his eyes. He wasn't smiling. In fact, he looked miserable. Instead of answering her, he just shrugged.

Rainbow Dash tried to shake it off. They'd decided to run the "three S's" first, with Sunset Shimmer flanking her on the right side. She'd pass the ball to Sunset Shimmer, and Sunset Shimmer would pass it back to her so she could throw to Twilight Sparkle, who would score. She couldn't worry about Forest Thunder right now—she wouldn't.

Orange Haze blew the whistle and Rainbow Dash took off. Forest Thunder was supposed to be blocking her, but within seconds she'd broken free of him, weaving her *S* up the field. She passed to Sunset Shimmer, and the rest of the play went just as it was supposed to. In less than a minute, Twilight Sparkle had scored. The stands erupted in cheers.

"First point to the GlitzyBlitzers!" Orange Haze announced.

Rainbow Dash joined her friends in the center of the field again. Applejack was giving her a funny look. "My guy barely blocked me," she whispered. "What's goin' on with them?"

"I don't know," Rainbow Dash said. "I'm

happy we scored, but you're right...something's off...."

For the next play, the boys had the ball. The girls ran one of their defensive favorites, a play they called the "Titans," because it was a mix of moves Rainbow Dash had seen that Blitzball team use. Within just a few minutes, Sunset Shimmer was able to steal the ball away from a boy named Duke and pass it to Applejack, who scored again. Orange Haze awarded them another point and the crowd cheered.

Comet stood on the sidelines. He looked furious. He'd been pacing back and forth the first two plays, and now he waved his hand in the air, calling a time-out. He pulled his team into a huddle. Rainbow Dash and her friends watched as they toweled off on the other side of the field. Comet was so loud they could hear bits and pieces of what he was saying.

"What was that?" he asked. He said something about "zero effort" and the boys being a "disappointment." While he was talking, a boy named Ivory leaned against his teammate. He looked exhausted.

"Comet must've been working them really hard," Sunset Shimmer said. "They look like they don't have anything left in them."

"I saw one of them fall asleep while he was on the bench...." Pinkie Pie added.

"If it keeps going like this, we'll win in a quarter of the time we thought we would," Rainbow Dash said.

"Is that really a bad thing?" Applejack asked. "I feel sorry for them, but I still don't feel sorry for Comet. He told you you couldn't join the team just because you're a girl."

Rainbow Dash knew Applejack had a point, but as she watched the boys slowly make their way back onto the field, she could tell they were all miserable. Comet had pulled one kid over and was yelling at him for a pass he'd missed.

She'd spent the last week determined to win the game. But was this fair? Did they really want to win like this?

CHAPTER 14

Throwing in the Towel

It was almost impossible to talk to the other team. Whenever the girls weren't running plays against them, the boys were on the sideline, being yelled at by Comet. Even though they'd scored two points, he didn't seem satisfied.

Rainbow Dash finally got her chance when

they were up 15–3. She and Forest Thunder were facing off against each other on the side of the field. Pinkie Pie was running the ball, and Rainbow Dash was about to dart out wide for the pass. Comet had called a time-out to talk to Ivory, so there were a few seconds before the game started again.

"What's wrong?" Rainbow Dash asked. "We know you can play better than this. What happened?"

"Comet happened," Forest Thunder said. "It's been awful. We've had two practices a day for the last two weeks and everyone's exhausted. It's like he thinks we should be professional-level Blitzball players already."

"You seem...burned out," Rainbow Dash said.

"We are. Everyone just wants to give up. A few of the guys have been talking about quitting after this scrimmage. I'm supposed to be the captain, but what am I gonna say? I hate it, too."

Rainbow Dash turned and watched Comet talking to Ivory. Comet was pointing his finger this way and that, his face twisted up as though he was mad. Ivory looked exhausted. Rainbow Dash knew Comet was a tough coach, but Forest Thunder was right. It was as if Comet thought high school students should be playing just as well as the Blitzers in the major league. Forest Thunder and his team had started playing the sport only last week!

"He's got it all wrong," Rainbow Dash said. "If you don't want to play like this, we shouldn't."

"What do you mean?" Forest Thunder asked.

"We should forfeit the game. Together. Now."

Forest Thunder's eyes went wide. Then, for the first time the entire game, he smiled. "You're serious...."

Rainbow Dash turned around and walked toward Orange Haze. She waved to Forest Thunder and her team to follow her. "Forest Thunder and I have decided we want to call the game. Let's say it was a tie. His team is exhausted, and it's no fun playing like this anyway."

"What?" Comet strode across the field, trying to stop Forest Thunder before he could say anything. "We're not calling anything. I don't call games."

"But I'm the captain. And I do," Forest Thunder said. "We're burned out, and no one wants to play anymore anyway. This is not some professional league where we're getting paid millions of dollars. This was supposed to be fun."

"Yeah, we quit," Ivory said, pulling off his helmet. "If this is what Blitzball is about, I don't want to be in the league."

A few of the other players pulled off their helmets, too. One boy actually plopped down on the grass, as if he'd been desperate to sit the whole game.

"I don't coach quitters. This was a once-in-a-lifetime opportunity, and you're going to be very sorry you passed it up," Comet said, turning to leave. He glared at Principal Celestia and Vice Principal Luna as he crossed the field toward the parking lot, as if it had been their fault.

CHAPTER 15

Game Changer

It wasn't until after Comet was gone that anyone said anything.

"I don't feel sorry..." one boy said. "I feel tired."

Another boy laughed. "Yeah, like I could sleep for days."

"Every muscle in my body hurts," a boy with a blue Mohawk said.

Principal Celestia, Vice Principal Luna, and Orange Haze gathered around the two teams. For a second, Rainbow Dash worried Principal Celestia might be mad, but she actually looked relieved. Both she and Vice Principal Luna were smiling.

"We're proud of you," Celestia said. "I hate to admit it, but that game was painful to watch. I wish I'd known Comet was working you all so hard. Competition is good, but not when it comes at so high a price."

"But now what do we do?" Forest Thunder asked. "We're never going to be allowed back in his high school Blitzball league."

"Yeah," Sunset Shimmer said. "I don't want to stop playing Blitzball just because it didn't work out with Comet. Can we find some other league to be a part of?"

Rainbow Dash looked at her friends' disappointed faces. They were right. They'd worked so hard and learned so much in the last two weeks. It would be a shame for all that to go to waste. But how were they going to play now?

Orange Haze studied the kids gathered in the crowd. He counted them up one by one and nodded. "Why not get an unofficial league going right here, right at Canterlot High? We have enough for two coed teams on this field. And if we're willing to train more players, we could have three, maybe four teams."

"We could offer it as an intramural sport," Vice Principal Luna said.

"I'd be happy to coach a team," Orange Haze said.

"That would be…incredible!" Pinkie Pie declared.

"A coed Blitzball team just for Canterlot High." Rainbow Dash said it out loud, just to hear how it sounded. It was even better than she could have imagined. They wouldn't be playing to win or playing to impress Comet. They'd be playing for fun. And to Rainbow Dash, that's what Blitzball was all about.

"Why don't we give these guys a break for the weekend?" Orange Haze said, nodding to the boys' team. "They look like they could use some rest. But next week, let's start practices. We could even have our first game next Friday."

"That's perfect," Rainbow Dash said. "I

don't want to have to wait too long to play Blitzball again."

"Me neither," Applejack said.

Rainbow Dash looked up into the stands, wondering if the crowd would be disappointed. They'd been promised a real Blitzball game, and halfway through, it had ended. But instead of being angry or annoyed, a group of girls was climbing down the bleachers. They strode out onto the field, right up to Rainbow Dash.

"Is it true?" a freshman with pink glasses asked. "Are you really forming a new Blitzball league just for Canterlot High?"

Rainbow Dash looked around at her friends and smiled. "We are!"

"Are girls allowed to join?" a sophomore with pigtails asked. She seemed nervous.

"You bet they are," Vice Principal Luna said.

"That's awesome!" the girl said. "Where do we sign up?"

As Rainbow Dash and Applejack wrote down the girls' names, they couldn't have been happier. Rainbow Dash kept picturing the new Canterlot league and all the cool, talented Blitzers they'd train. The fun practices they'd have, the stands packed with people cheering for them. People would come from all over Equestria to see them play. And when they did, everyone would know how fierce girl Blitzers could be.

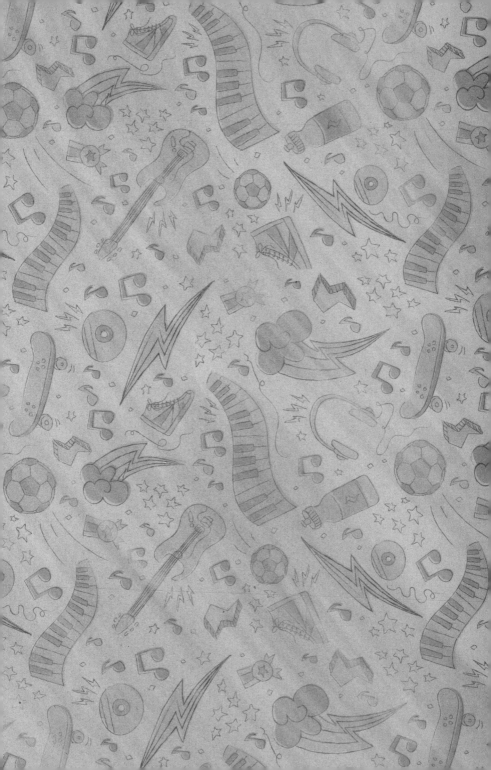

CHAPTER 16

Coed Harmony

Rainbow Dash ran the ball up the field, dribbling it twice. She did a graceful turn, then passed it to Forest Thunder, who took it another few feet before looking for someone to throw to. Pinkie Pie was stuck behind a massive boy named Maple Tree, so she did the "leaping lizard." She jumped out behind him just in time to catch it. They raced up the field together, using more of their signature moves, and within minutes Ivory had scored a goal for them.

"Flawless!" Rarity called out from the bench. "We're starting to look like real professionals."

It was their last practice before the big scrimmage, and Rainbow Dash couldn't believe how good their team had gotten. It was sad to split up the GlitzyBlitzers, but Pinkie Pie, Applejack, Rarity, and she had joined up with three of the boys to form the new team. They called themselves the Zips. They'd practiced together for only four days, but in that time they'd gotten so close. The best part was they still got to play with their friends whenever they wanted. The other team had just come by on Tuesday for an unofficial practice game.

"That's a wrap!" Vice Principal Luna said. "I think we're more than prepared for the big scrimmage tomorrow. Rest up and get ready to have fun!"

Rainbow Dash and Applejack grabbed their duffel bags from the sidelines. Forest Thunder and his friends came over to them, their helmets tucked underneath their arms. "I don't know if I can rest," Forest Thunder said. "I'm too excited about tomorrow."

"We were talking about going over to Tomato Pie around eight. We wanted to get some pasta before the big game," Rainbow Dash said. "Like, an unofficial pasta party. All our friends are meeting us there."

"A pasta party?" Ivory asked.

"If you eat lots of carbs before a big game, it's supposed to give you extra energy," Applejack explained.

"It'll be like the opposite of last time." Ivory laughed.

Forest Thunder looked at Rainbow Dash and smiled, a twinkle in his eye. "Yeah, we'll definitely be there. Save a seat for us!"

As they walked away, Rarity grabbed Rainbow Dash's arm. "He definitely likes you."

Rainbow Dash just waved her away. She didn't have time to wonder if Forest Thunder liked her or not. Sure, he was cute and nice, but the big game was tomorrow and she didn't want to get distracted. What was more important than that?

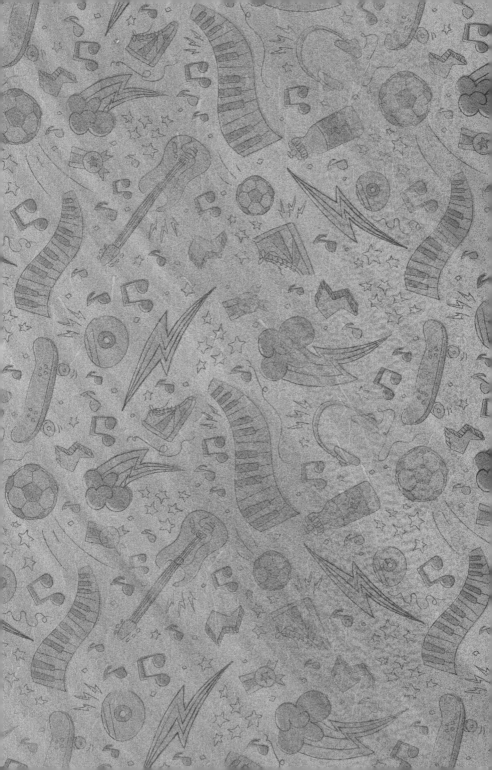

CHAPTER

17

Pasta Partying

That night, Tomato Pie was packed with people. It was the kind of place that had red-and-white-gingham everything—tablecloths, curtains, napkins, and placemats. The food was served on dishes the size of a person's head. Rainbow Dash and her friends had gotten a long table in the back of the restaurant, and it was now covered with half-eaten piles of pasta and torn loaves of bread. Everyone had taken this whole "eat a lot of carbs" thing pretty seriously.

"Did you need some more spaghetti?" Sunset Shimmer asked. She held up a heaping plateful.

"You shouldn't be so nice to us," Applejack said, taking it from her. "It makes me feel sorry we're goin' to have to beat you tomorrow."

"You wish!" Sunset Shimmer laughed gamely. "The Slammers are going to win, no question about it."

It had been like that all night. Now that the scrimmage was tomorrow, Rainbow Dash and her team kept going back and forth, talking about who would win. It was all in good fun, and no one was taking it too seriously, but Rainbow Dash did think they had the best chance. Was the other team really as good as they were? As quick and as graceful?

Forest Thunder and the rest of the boys appeared in the front entrance. Forest Thunder looked as if he might explode with excitement. He was holding something in his hand, waving it around for everyone in the restaurant to see. It wasn't until he got closer that Rainbow Dash realized it was a newspaper.

"The *Canterlot Gazette*!" he said, putting it down on the table. "Did you see this? It's today's edition! Look who made the front page!"

There was a story on the right-hand side with the headline: CANTERLOT HIGH SPLITS FROM BEEHIVE BLITZERS'S COMET TO CREATE

COED BLITZBALL LEAGUE. Rainbow Dash picked up the paper and started reading. It told the whole story, start to finish, complete with her pushing for the league to be coed. It talked about how much pressure Comet had put on the boys' team and how everyone had ultimately decided to make the Blitzball league intramural. It had a long quote from Comet and two more from Vice Principal Luna and Principal Celestia. Comet didn't seem happy. . . .

"*'Since its debut twenty years ago, Blitzball has always been an all-male sport. I'm a person who believes in tradition. I wasn't going to compromise or cave to pressure,'*" Rainbow Dash read, furrowing her brows. "Wow, he still thinks he's right, huh?"

"Read the quote from Vice Principal Luna," Forest Thunder said. He leaned over, pointing to a line a few paragraphs down.

"'Rainbow Dash embodies what we want our students to be,'" Rarity read. "'She inspires others to do their best and to not take no for an answer, no matter where that no comes from.'"

Rainbow Dash felt her face flush. It was nice to hear Luna say those things about her; it just was weird to hear Rarity say it with both teams there. She could feel everyone watching her.

"Look," Rainbow Dash said, pointing to the bottom. "They gave all the details of the first game tomorrow. They're encouraging all of Canterlot to come out and support us."

"Seems like our little game just got a lot bigger," Ivory said.

As they passed around the newspaper,

everyone was laughing and smiling. Ivory kept teasing Twilight Sparkle that his team was going to win, and Sunset Shimmer was still coming up with last-minute plays, scribbling them down on a piece of paper. She and Fluttershy kept passing it back and forth to each other. The music was blasting over the restaurant speakers, and Rarity and Pinkie Pie shimmied in their seats. Rainbow Dash looked around at all her friends, new and old. She'd never been more certain that Comet was wrong. *This* was true team spirit; *this* was showing up with your whole heart. *This* was what Blitzball was all about....

CHAPTER 18

The Big Day

"My, oh, my," Rarity said, peeking out the gym door. "That crowd is for us?"

The stands by the football field were packed. There must've been a few hundred people there, all with signs and pom-poms, ready to root on the teams. Someone had a sign that said: COED BLITZBALL IS THE ONLY

BLITZBALL I'LL WATCH, and another person had one that said: LET GIRLS BLITZBALL! Almost everyone was in Canterlot High's school colors—gold and blue.

"I guess people really liked that story," Forest Thunder said.

But Rainbow Dash couldn't think about the crowd now. She knew they were in an intramural league, but her competitive nature had already kicked in. She wanted to win today.

"Everyone ready?" she asked, glancing at the line of players behind her. They were all in their new Blitzball outfits. Rarity hadn't had time to make the official uniforms yet, so they'd pulled together gold tops and bottoms from a local store. Applejack had found this cool gold tape that they'd used to decorate their helmets.

"Ready!" a few voices called out.

"I said…is everyone ready?" Rainbow Dash asked again, this time with more excitement in her voice.

"Yeah!!" everyone cheered.

They trotted out of the gym and toward the field, the team following Rainbow Dash in one straight line. The other team was already on the sidelines. They wore head-to-toe blue, and they'd even written *the Slammers* in script across their helmets. As soon as the crowd saw the Zips coming toward them, it went wild.

"Let's huddle up," Rainbow Dash said. Vice Principal Luna came into the circle, wrapping her arms around Rainbow Dash's and Rarity's shoulders. Rainbow Dash continued, "We've come so far in such a short amount of time. I'm so proud of us. Let's play hard today and show everyone what coed Blitzball is about!"

The team put their hands together in the center of the circle, then did a quick cheer.

"I'd say, 'Make me proud,'" Vice Principal Luna began. "But I'm already so proud of you all. So I guess...make me prouder!"

"We will!" Applejack said as she darted onto the field.

The Slammers had won the coin toss, so they had the ball first. Rarity and Sea Cloud, a tall, skinny boy from Comet's original team, were sitting on the bench to start. The rest of the Zips were out on the field, ready to face off against their friends. Rainbow Dash stood in front of Twilight Sparkle. She narrowed her eyes, trying to look fierce.

"Catch me if you can." Twilight Sparkle winked.

Seconds later, the whistle split the air. Flax, a boy from the other team, ran up the field with the ball, weaving between players. He passed to Fluttershy, who kept eyeing Twilight Sparkle. Rainbow Dash knew she wanted to pass to her, but she couldn't let that happen. Fluttershy dribbled twice, then a third time, but then she was stuck. She swiveled back and forth and finally just chucked the ball at Twilight Sparkle. Rainbow Dash leaped to the side and caught it before Twilight Sparkle had the chance.

The whistle sounded again, and Rainbow Dash went back into the center of the field. Pinkie Pie was running the ball this time. Now that she was super focused, she was one of the fastest players on the team. She passed to Applejack, who passed to Ivory. He let Rainbow Dash get within feet of the goal before passing to her. She turned and shot it before anyone could block her. It swished into the back of the net!

The crowd went crazy. Everyone in the stands was on their feet, waving and cheering. As Rainbow Dash ran back into the center of the field to start the next play, she glanced up and saw a familiar face. Comet was in the very back row. He was watching the game intently, focused on the players' every move.

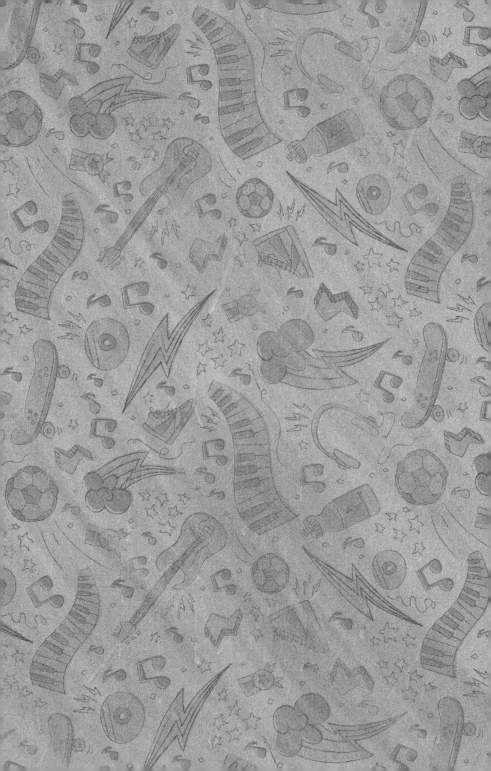

CHAPTER 19

A New Game

What was Comet doing here? Hadn't he quit? Hadn't he acted as though Rainbow Dash were offending the honor of Blitzball players everywhere? She tried to push it out of her mind as she took off, helping Forest Thunder run the ball up the field.

By the time the first half ended, Rainbow Dash's team was up by two points. The competition had been fierce, and for a while it looked as though Twilight Sparkle's team might win. The boys on her team had used the under/over block three times, and it worked perfectly.

The ref blew the whistle again, starting the halftime show. Because it had turned into such a big event, Principal Celestia had asked the school dance team to perform. Music blasted as they cartwheeled and somersaulted onto the field. They took a V formation and started grooving to the beat.

Rainbow Dash got water and toweled off, trying to stay focused. As she was running some of the plays for the second half through her head, she felt a tap on her shoulder. She assumed it was Vice Principal Luna, but when she turned around Comet was standing next to her. He was smiling.

"I thought you didn't want girls playing Blitzball," Rainbow Dash said. Her friends noticed what was happening. A few had turned around, watching as they spoke to each other.

"That was certainly what I thought," Comet said. "Because it hadn't really been done before. But you and your friends are some of the best players out there. I don't know…I'm starting to think a coed league makes sense."

"It sounds like what you want to say," Applejack offered, butting into the conversation, "is sorry. And that you were wrong."

Comet nodded, his expression suddenly serious. "I *was* wrong. And I didn't come here to ask to coach the team. I wanted to tell you I'm going to start that training league you spoke about. That way any girl who wants to play Blitzball can."

"That is fantastic news," Vice Principal Luna said. It seemed as if everyone was listening to their conversation now. A few of the players from the other team had come around to their side of the field, too.

"It's more fun," Comet said, pointing to the coed team. "And someone really smart once told me that was what Blitzball was all about."

As the dance team ended the halftime show, Comet disappeared back into the crowd. He gave Principal Celestia some information about the new training program, telling her he'd help out with any of the middle schoolers who were interested. Then he was gone.

During the entire second half, Rainbow Dash felt as if she were flying. She ran faster than she had before, and she didn't overthink any of her plays. Everything was effortless. Even the hoots and cheers of the crowd seemed far away. By the time the game was ending, she didn't care about winning. She would've been happy if the game had gone on for another hour. She just wanted to keep playing.

Forest Thunder tossed her the ball. "This should be it," he said. "We're only one more goal away from winning. You should do the honors...."

"Should we do the 'whizby'?" Rainbow Dash asked. She was talking about one of the plays she and Forest Thunder had come up with together. It involved one runner taking the ball all the way to the goal with only short, quick passes to avoid breaking the rules.

"Let's do it." Forest Thunder smiled.

This was it. The last play on their first coed Blitzball game. And she was going to score the last point. Her stomach did a quick somersault, and her palms began to sweat. She couldn't slip up now. Was she ready?

As soon as the whistle sounded, she sprinted as fast as she could. She dribbled three times and did a quick pass and pass back with Forest Thunder. Then she dribbled three more times and did a quick pass with Pinkie Pie. When she was close to the goal, she exchanged the ball with Ivory, then she got as close as she could and slammed it into the net. It hit the back with a glorious *swoosh*!

Everyone in the stands stood up, their arms raised in excitement. A group of freshman girls started chanting her name. Her team rushed in around her, offering hugs and congratulations.

Rainbow Dash took it all in. Her friends' smiling faces, her heart pounding in her chest. She didn't think she'd ever felt so happy in her entire life. This was what it was like to be a famous Blitzball player. To do the thing you love every day, to play with everything you have, to hear people cheer for you.

"Did we make you *prouder*?" Rainbow Dash said when she spotted Vice Principal Luna in the crowd.

"The *proudest*." Luna smiled.

Rainbow Dash smiled as the team took their first victory lap around the field.

Rainbow Dash's Signature Style

Rainbow Dash is an athleisure superstar! "Athleisure" is a new clothing trend where athletic and leisure clothing live together in all kinds of cool and comfortable ways. This is a world where sneakers are the best footwear and comfort is the ultimate fashion statement; a world where workout pants are the name of the game.

This is a world where Rainbow Dash reigns supreme. She lives in **comfy but fashionable** clothing, and she brings her own colorful vibe to the table. She is a girl who never met a pair of **workout pants** she didn't love, but she won't stick to just any old basic black pant. Her workout gear has to be special. She rocks **bright, bold colors** and **eye-catching patterns**— never "basic" anything. And to make her pants really pop, she like to pair them with a great statement-making jacket. Instead of a simple zip-up hoodie, she opts for a **satin bomber** or a **varsity jacket**. These trendy tops pull her whole **fashionable-yet-practical** look together.

Even though she has a **tomboy vibe**, Rainbow Dash still enjoys accessorizing. She rocks *metallic accents* and *jewelry*. She prefers to keep it *simple and cool* instead of overly girly and feminine. You'll never catch her in a fussy statement necklace…no way. And you certainly will never see her sprinting down the street in heels. Why? Because not only does she care about style—she cares about comfort. So instead of heels, she struts in athletic *sneakers* and *high-tops*. But as always, to keep her look as bright and colorful as she is, Rainbow Dash opts for a blinged-out high-top or a sequined sneaker.

Are you a Rainbow Dash?

Let's talk about how you can recreate her looks with some key pieces.

Statement Sneakers

First, you need some cool kicks. Sneakers and high-tops are a must. But do *not* go for the basics! Look for silver, gold, or sequined options. These will be the basis for all your looks. These metallic choices can go with anything and everything. They are a great neutral with a little something extra.

Shutterstock.com/Ragnarock

Colorful Workout Pants

Second, you need some standout leggings or pants. Bold colors, graphic prints, or shiny metallics are all great choices that would get the Rainbow Dash seal of approval.

The Perfect Jacket

Next, you need a great jacket. Look for colors, prints, cool fabrics or textures, or just something that screams *fun*! Keep in mind what you have on the bottom. Do you have a ton of color and prints? If so, keep the jacket a little simpler. If you have a simple color palette on the bottom, then get color crazy with the top.

Shutterstock.com/Petar Djordjevic

Simple but Bold Accessories

Finally, pick a little bling to finish off your look. If you have pierced ears, look for a rebellious ear climber or maybe a creative set of mismatched earrings. If a necklace is more your thing, remember that *less is more*. A lightning bolt or bold geometric shape is cool. Keep it simple and sleek, and let your colorful clothing be the star.

Shutterstock.com/Ukki Studio

Can you spot the pieces of atheleisure clothing in Rainbow Dash's wardrobe?

Shutterstock.com: Pratt Digitdesv, Kiwont, Tarzhanova, NYS, elenvovsky, Anastasiia Krizhanska, Gordana Sermek

Now it's your turn to style Rainbow Dash! Draw her a new outfit!

Design your own stylish
Blitzball uniform!

Write about your own personal style.

What would be Rainbow Dash's biggest fashion Dos and Don'ts?

DOs

DON'Ts

Can you create three outfits for Rainbow Dash using the pieces shown?

Time to go to the mall! Fill out your Rainbow Dash-inspired shopping list!

-
-
-
-
-
-
-

Write about something that inspires your style!